FRASER BEAR

Fraser

● ● ●

Maggie de Vries

Illustrated by **Renné Benoit**

A CUB'S LIFE
Bear

GREYSTONE BOOKS
D&M PUBLISHERS INC.
Vancouver/Toronto/Berkeley

The publisher gratefully acknowledges the enthusiastic support of Rocky Mountaineer and

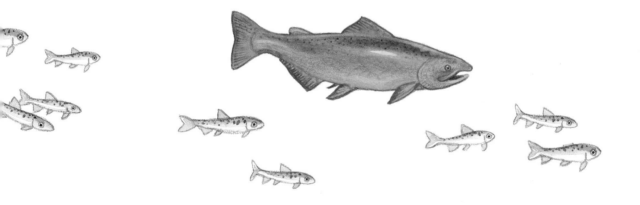

*the Pacific Salmon Foundation in the creation of **Fraser Bear**.*

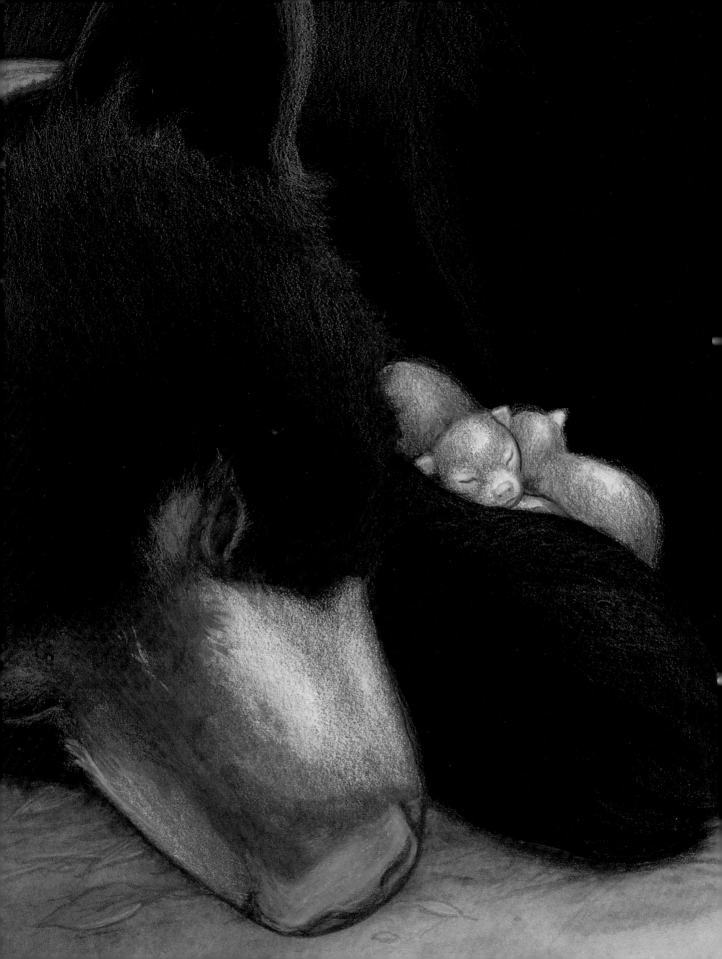

JANUARY

Deep in their den, two baby bears snuggle against their mother's belly, drinking her rich, warm milk. Tiny and hairless and blind, they are as happy as they can be. As they drink, they make a humming sound, like the buzzing of bees.

Far away, in the ocean, thousands of chinook salmon begin their long journey home.

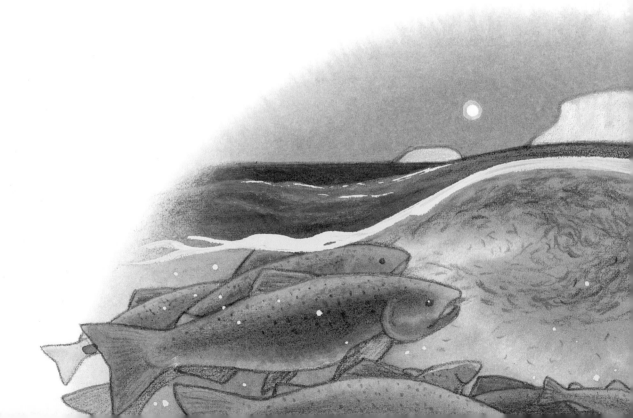

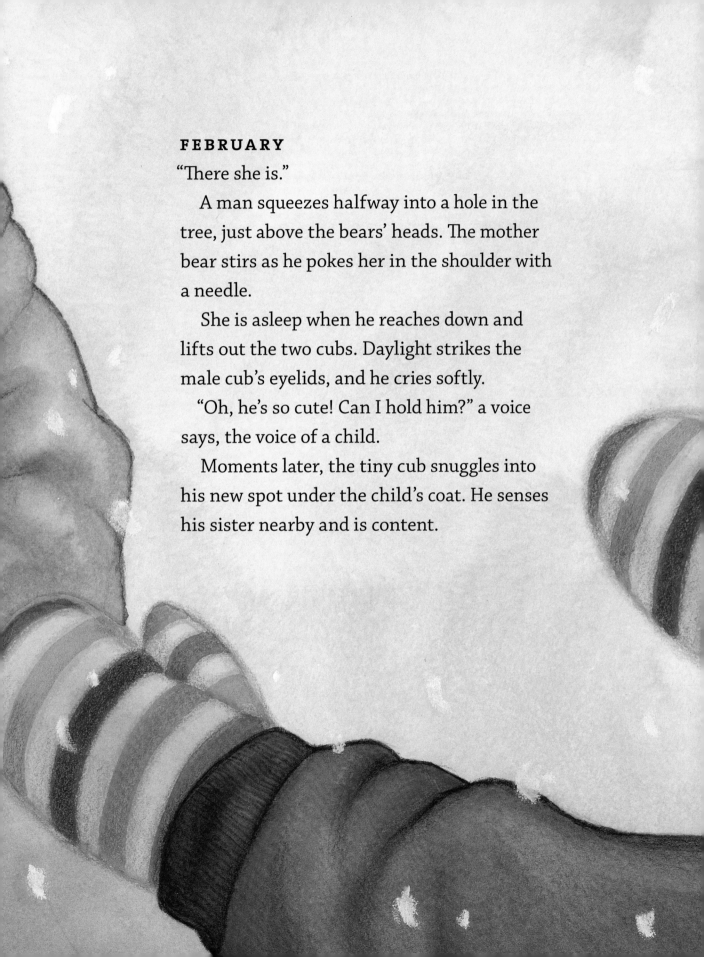

FEBRUARY

"There she is."

A man squeezes halfway into a hole in the tree, just above the bears' heads. The mother bear stirs as he pokes her in the shoulder with a needle.

She is asleep when he reaches down and lifts out the two cubs. Daylight strikes the male cub's eyelids, and he cries softly.

"Oh, he's so cute! Can I hold him?" a voice says, the voice of a child.

Moments later, the tiny cub snuggles into his new spot under the child's coat. He senses his sister nearby and is content.

The child peers at the female cub. "Samantha," she says. "I name you Samantha. And you," she says, turning to the male bear, "I name you Fraser. Fraser Bear."

The man changes the mother bear's collar, weighs and measures her, and returns her to the tree. He places the cubs against their mother's chest.

It is time to go. The child walks away as slowly as she can.

One day, she hopes, she will see Fraser and Samantha again.

APRIL

Fraser opens his eyes for the first time. His sister
looks back at him.

After the bears have a feed and a snooze, their
mother shoves her front feet and her nose under
Fraser and pushes him up and out—into the world!

Moonlight washes over the small bear.

He shakes his head and breathes the chill
night air. Until now he has known only the smell
of bear. The new smells are sharp and clean. Snow.
And trees—pine, spruce.

He listens. An owl hoots. In the distance, a
wolf howls.

The snow is cold under Fraser's paws. With
the tip of one paw, he touches the crisp edge of
a shadow.

His sister shoves past. Fraser turns and gives
her a good cuff. Their mother watches as the cubs
fall over and over each other in the snow.

Early next morning, far away, boats go out
to sea. Men and women lower their nets.

MAY

The melt is on. Water rushes down the mountains.

The cubs are always hungry. Day after day, they follow their mother in search of new growth. They climb for it, up bare, slippery slopes. Many times a day, they stop to drink their mother's milk.

The mother bear is even hungrier than her cubs. She watches for food, and for danger.

Nearer now, the salmon that have survived the journey swim into the wide, muddy mouth of the Fraser River.

JUNE

One morning, Fraser's mother spots a moose calf, all alone.

She huffs her cubs up a tree. Fraser is curious and stops, but a swat on the rear sends him scrambling after his sister.

The cubs peer down from the branches as their mother stalks the calf. But the calf sees her and bawls. Suddenly its mother appears, sharp hooves raised against the great hungry bear. Ears back, Fraser's mother retreats as the calf presses tight against its mother's side.

JULY

Fraser falls onto his back and pulls a huckleberry branch down to his mouth.

A sound. His eyes fly open . . . and he stares into the face of an enormous bear.

Silent now, the bear steps closer.

Crying loudly, Fraser rolls to his feet and runs up the first tree in his path. The tree is small. It bends. Fraser clings to his bendy branch and cries.

The huge bear rakes Fraser's body
with his claws. Fraser squeals and drops
to the ground. The bear raises his paw
for another blow.

A furious roar stops the paw in midair. The bear's big head whips around.

And Fraser's mother is there, shoving her body between cub and bear. The male bear's anger is no match for hers. He retreats a pace or two and lumbers away.

Samantha creeps backward down a nearby tree. Fraser lies still, moaning softly. His mother sniffs at his wound and licks and licks.

The fish reach the rapids in the Fraser Canyon. A cement ladder built under the water helps them pass through. On they swim.

AUGUST / SEPTEMBER

The berries in July were good, but the berries in August are better. Fraser loves the blueberries best. Insects are everywhere—ants and beetles and their grubs. Soon there will be nuts. The bears stuff themselves. They must grow fat or they will die before the spring comes.

One day, the mother leads her cubs to the river's rocky shore. Fraser stares. The water is alive! It squirms. It wriggles. Fraser has never seen water like this before.

The spawning grounds at last! Female salmon sweep their tails to make redds, or nests, for their eggs. Males gather. The river fills with fish.

The cubs watch as their mother springs. Soon
she grasps a thrashing salmon in her teeth. Fraser
spots a fish and jumps after it. His teeth clank
together, empty. Nearby, his sister does no better.
  Their mother grunts to her cubs to follow, and
the bears make their way into the woods to feast
on her catch undisturbed.

The female salmon release their eggs. The males release a cloud of milt over them. Fertilized, the eggs drift down into the redds.

Their work done, their bodies weak, the fish
live on for some time to protect their eggs. At
last, though, each chinook must die. Their bodies
become food for many other creatures. And for
the forest itself.

Fraser has no trouble catching dead fish. And he learns that dead fish come alive in a few days with maggots. Extra-delicious!

He eats and eats, nuts and bugs and berries, as well as fish. Under his coat, fat piles on fat. Soon it will be time to sleep.

OCTOBER

Fraser's mother has found a den among the roots of a fallen tree. Fraser and Samantha help her line it with leaves and grass.

Weeks more of eating—mostly nuts now, and squirrels' caches when they can find them. Snow comes. The den's entrance is hidden by a great white drift. The cubs squeeze in after their mother, curl up against her belly, and go to sleep.

At the bottom of the river, eyes grow inside the eggs. Later, the eggs hatch. Buried safe in the riverbed, the hatchlings feed on their yolk sacs.

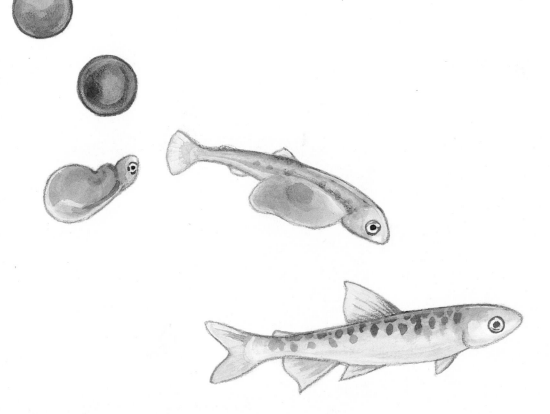

MAY

Until the time comes for Fraser to leave his mother, he does not know that he will go.

One day, though, just before his second summer, Fraser wanders off in search of the next green patch. His mother watches as he disappears from view.

Fraser finds a rotten log and flips it over, lapping up bugs and tugging at fat grubs with his teeth.

When he is done, he looks for a good tree. Moments later, he settles into the crook of two strong branches ten meters off the ground. Fraser closes his eyes for a nap, alone for the first time in his life.

Last year's hatchlings, now the size of stubby pencils, swim for the sea.

JUNE

Fraser hunts for leaves and berries and grubs.

He stops. Something smells sweet and delicious. Fraser follows his nose until he comes out into the open, and there they are—buzzing boxes! They are behind a fence, but he has pushed down fences before.

He rears up, sending the fence crashing, and falls back with a loud bellow. The fence has attacked him!

Fraser will be fully grown and a father before he gets his first taste of honey-coated bee grubs.

SEPTEMBER

Fish have arrived at the river again! Down Fraser
goes and up he comes, but the fish slip by. He
jumps. He dives. The fish slither from his teeth.

There—a huge salmon, ragged from its journey.
This one does not slip away.

From a rubber raft downstream, people watch.
One is the child, older now. "Look, Dad," she says.
"That's Fraser. See? He caught a fish!"
Fraser is pulling himself ashore, heading for
the woods with his prize.
"Could be," her father says. "But you can't be sure."
The child watches her bear and smiles.

OCTOBER

Fraser is fat—fat on berries and bugs, nuts and fish. He rarely remembers his mother and sister now.

Back in September, before the first snow fell, he found and prepared his den.

Now he makes his way inside and turns around. He lies down and presses his behind against the back wall. Drawing his legs close to his body, Fraser Bear takes a deep breath.

And falls asleep.

BEAR SAFETY

In this story, the child holds bear cubs. She is allowed to do this because she is with her father, a biologist, who has been specially trained to handle bears in a safe way. People who do not have this training should never approach a bear. This rule protects both people and bears. To find out more about safety in bear country, look at www.bearsmart.com.

ABOUT BLACK BEARS

· Newborn black bears weigh about 300 g (10 ounces). They are hairless and blind, as their eyes are sealed shut until they are a month old.

· Cubs spend almost half of their first year in trees, where they are safe. Sometimes mothers feed their cubs in trees.

· Grown male bears live alone. Females stay with their mothers longer, sometimes for several years.

· Black bears live for about twenty years. Females have their first cubs when they are three or four years old.

· Male bears have been known to kill cubs.

· To prepare for hibernation, bears must eat up to triple their usual amount of food. Unlike most animals that hibernate, bears wake easily during hibernation. Female bears give birth during hibernation.

· Honey farmers use electric fences to keep bears out of their hives. The bears love both the honey and the bee grubs.

ABOUT THE CHINOOK
SALMON OF THE FRASER RIVER

- The chinook is one of seven kinds of salmon. The others are sockeye, pink, chum, coho, steelhead, and cutthroat. Chinook are the biggest.
- Chinook swim as far as 12,000 km (7,456 miles) in their lifetimes.
- From the time they turn back east along the Aleutian Islands to the time they reach the mouth of the Fraser, chinook double in size. On their way up the river, they lose up to one-third of their body mass.
- The chinook's journey up the Fraser is the second-longest spawning journey in the world, at 1,300 km (807 miles).
- The biggest chinook ever recorded weighed 57 kg (126 pounds).
- Each year, fewer and fewer wild chinook salmon return to the Fraser River to spawn. When salmon are scarce, bears can starve. Bears and salmon need our help if they are to survive.

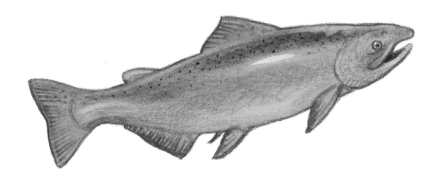

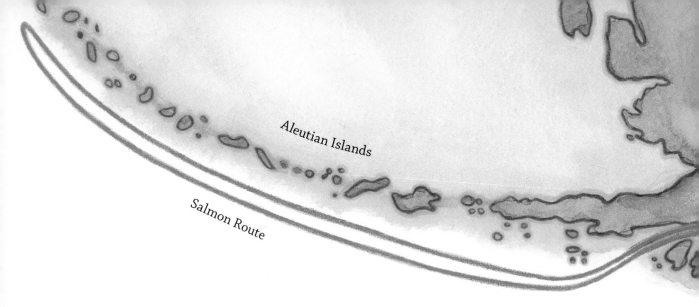

Aleutian Islands

Salmon Route

GLOSSARY

cache A collection of nuts and other food that a squirrel or other animal sets aside in a hiding place in preparation for winter.

fertilize To make an egg able to develop into new life. Male fish do this by releasing milt over the eggs that a female releases.

hibernation Sleeping in dens during the winter, as black bears and some other animals do.

lumber To walk in a slow, clumsy way.

maggots Fly larvae. They are nourishing food for bears.

milt A substance that male fish release to fertilize eggs.

redd The nest that a female salmon digs by sweeping her tale in the gravel riverbed.

spawn To release eggs or milt.

yolk sac A yolk-filled pouch attached to a new fish when it hatches from the egg.

ALASKA

Alaska Range

• Anchorage

Mackenzie
Mountains

*Gulf
of Alaska*

Juneau
•

Alaskan Panhandle

BRITISH
COLUMBIA

R o c k y   M o u n t a i n s

Prince
George •

Fraser Bear's birthplace
• Mount Robson
• Valemount

Fraser River

Vancouver
•

Hell's Gate

Victoria —

ACKNOWLEDGMENTS

Special thanks to Rocky Mountaineer for assisting me in the research for this book by sending me on the Fraser Discovery train journey, which followed the Fraser River all the way from its headwaters. Thanks to Chad Brealey of the Pacific Salmon Foundation for suggesting Mount Robson as the setting and chinook as the fish, and for his invaluable assistance in reading the manuscript for factual accuracy. Any errors that remain are mine. Thanks also to everyone at the Valemount Visitor Centre and the Mount Robson Provincial Park Visitor Centre who shared their local knowledge about black bears and chinook.

Thank you, Kathy, for your editorial guidance and for your enthusiasm for the story. Thanks also to Rob and Nancy at Greystone for thinking of me for this project, and for bringing Renné and me together again.

Maggie de Vries

To Roland—MdV
For Uncle Moel—RB

10 11 12 13 14   5 4 3 2 1

Greystone Books
An imprint of D&M Publishers Inc.
2323 Quebec Street, Suite 201
Vancouver, BC Canada V5T 4S7
www.greystonebooks.com

Library and Archives Canada Cataloguing in Publication
De Vries, Maggie
Fraser bear : a cub's adventure / Maggie de Vries ; illustrated by Renné Benoit.

ISBN 978-1-55365-521-3

1. Bear cubs—Juvenile literature. 2. Black bear—Juvenile literature.
3. Black bear—Food—British Columbia—Juvenile literature. 4. Pacific salmon—
British Columbia—Fraser River—Juvenile literature. I. Benoit, Renné II. Title.

QL795.B4D48 2010   j599.78′5   C2009-906308-5

Editing by Kathy Vanderlinden
Jacket design by Heather Pringle and Jessica Sullivan
Text design by Jessica Sullivan
Jacket illustration by Renné Benoit
Printed and bound in Canada by Friesens
Printed on paper that comes from sustainable forests
managed under the Forest Stewardship Council
Distributed in the U.S. by Publishers Group West

We gratefully acknowledge the financial support of the Canada Council for the Arts, the British Columbia Arts Council, the Province of British Columbia through the Book Publishing Tax Credit, and the Government of Canada through the Book Publishing Industry Development Program (BPIDP) for our publishing activities.

Mixed Sources
Cert no. SW-COC-001271
© 1996 FSC
FSC

PACIFIC SALMON FOUNDATION

The Pacific Salmon Foundation was created in 1987 as an independent, non-governmental organization to protect, conserve, and rebuild wild Pacific salmon populations in the Pacific Northwest. The foundation raises money and makes grants to volunteer organizations that work on behalf of salmon in rivers, streams, and watersheds across British Columbia.

ROCKY MOUNTAINEER

Providing the world's best train experience, the Rocky Mountaineer journeys in daylight through the majestic Canadian Rockies. Rocky Mountaineer supports the preservation of natural salmon habitats through the work of the Pacific Salmon Foundation.